Jacqueline Wilson
The Monster
Story-Teller

Illustrated by Nick Sharratt

CORGI PUPS

THE MONSTER STORY-TELLER
A CORGI PUPS BOOK 978 0 552 56481 6

First published in Great Britain by Doubleday,
an imprint of Random House Children's Publishers UK
A Random House Group Company

Doubleday edition published 1997
First Corgi Pups edition published 1997
Corgi Pups edition reissued 2008

This edition published 2011

5 7 9 10 8 6

Text copyright © Jacqueline Wilson, 1995
Illustrations copyright © Nick Sharratt, 1996

The right of Jacqueline Wilson to be identified as the author
of this work has been asserted in accordance with the
Copyright, Designs and Patents Act 1988.

Set in Bembo Infant MT Standard

Corgi Pups Books are published by Random House Children's Publishers UK
61–63 Uxbridge Road, London W5 5SA

www.**randomhousechildrens**.co.uk

Addresses for companies within The Random House Group Limited
can be found at: www.**randomhouse**.co.uk/offices.htm

THE RANDOM HOUSE GROUP Limited Reg. No. 954009

A CIP catalogue record for this book is available
from the British Library.

Printed and bound in China

For Sean William MacLahlan

CONTENTS

Series Reading Consultant: Prue Goodwin
Reading and Language Information Centre,
University of Reading

Chapter One

Natalie was fed up.

The class were doing a project on flying.

She had made a big bird but his wings went wonky. He wouldn't fly.

Natalie talked to her friends.

"What did you do on Saturday?" Natalie asked.

"I went swimming," said Clare.

"I went to McDonald's," said Zoe.

"I went to the football match," said Lee.

"I went shopping with my nan," said Clive. "She gave me five pounds. And she bought me chocolates. Yum yum."

"Do you want to hear what I did on Saturday?" said Natalie. "First I went swimming and there were real dolphins in the pool and they gave me a ride. Then I went to McDonald's and I had twenty Big Macs and twenty strawberry milk shakes. And then

I went to this football match and I was the mascot and I scored a goal and everyone cheered. And then I went shopping with my nan and she gave me fifty pounds and lots and lots and lots of chocolates."

"How many chocolates?" said Clive.

"Natalie's telling stories, silly,"
said Lee.

"Settle down, children!" said
Mr Hunter. "Natalie, get on with
your work and stop telling
stories. It's not story-time until
this afternoon – when we're
going to have a special treat."

"I want a special treat now,"
Natalie muttered. "This is boring,
boring, boring."

She sighed.

She stretched.

She looked up at the window.
She looked at the plant in the
pot on the window sill.

And the plant in the pot moved.

Natalie blinked.

The plant in the pot moved again. Upwards!

Was the plant in the pot flying?

Then Natalie saw!

The plant in the pot wasn't flying.

It was the saucer.

It was an ordinary flower-patterned saucer. But today it had grown wings.

"Of course!" said Natalie. "It's
a flying saucer!"

She went to have a closer look.

There was a little creature
standing in the saucer.

Was it an ant?

"A flying ant!" Natalie giggled.

It wasn't an ant.

It was a very, very, very tiny
monster.

It had wild hair and pointy
teeth and sharp claws and a long
tail.

But it didn't look fierce. It
looked friendly.

"Hello!" said Natalie.

"Hello!" said the tiny monster.

"Can you speak up a bit?" said Natalie. "I can't hear you properly."

"I'm shouting!" said the tiny monster. "Can you speak down a bit? You're hurting my ears."

"Is it your flying saucer?"
Natalie whispered, so softly her
lips scarcely moved.

The tiny monster nodded
proudly.

"Want to see me do twirlie-
whirlies?" he said.

"You bet!" said Natalie.

The tiny monster tapped his teeny foot.

The saucer flapped its little wings and whizzed round and round in the air. The plant's leaves waved wildly.

The tiny monster waved too as he circled Natalie's head, round and round until she got dizzy.

The plant wobbled and wobbled until . . .

. . . it tipped right off the saucer and crashed onto the classroom floor!

"Oh help!" said the tiny monster.

"Oh help!" said Natalie. "What's Mr Hunter going to say?"

Chapter Two

Mr Hunter said plenty.
"You naughty girl, Natalie!

What were you doing over by
the window? Did you knock that
plant over on purpose?"

"No! It wasn't me," said Natalie.

"It was me!" said the tiny
monster, flying his saucer behind
Natalie.

"Look at the mess on the floor!
Go and fetch a dustpan and
brush from the store cupboard,
Natalie," said Mr Hunter. "And
take that silly smile off your face.
It isn't funny."

Natalie couldn't help smiling.
The tiny monster was tickling the
back of her neck with his weeny
claws.

Natalie hurried out of the classroom.

The flying saucer went with her, whirling round her head.

"Where are you going?" shouted the tiny monster.

"To fetch the dustpan and brush," said Natalie.

"Boring, boring, boring," said the tiny monster. "Come flying with me instead. Jump up on my saucer."

"I can't," said Natalie. "I'm much too big. I'd smash the saucer. And squash you."

"I can make you small," said the tiny monster. "Hold my hand."

Natalie held out her great big hand. The tiny monster held out his weeny little paw.

Then Natalie started shrinking!

She felt as if she were being rubbed with very powerful magic soap.

She got smaller and smaller and smaller until she was exactly the same size as the tiny monster. Only he didn't look tiny now.

The monster's hair was very
wild.

His teeth were very pointy.
His claws were very sharp.
His tail was very long.
But he still didn't look fierce.
He looked friendly.

"Let's fly," said the monster.
"Shall we go fast?"

"You bet!" said Natalie.

The monster tapped his paw
and the wings flapped very fast
indeed. The flying saucer whizzed
way down the school corridor.

"Aaaaah!" said Natalie.

"This is easy-peasy slowcoach stuff," said the monster, showing off like mad. "Let's go outside."

Natalie nodded.

She didn't have any breath left for talking.

They flew very fast across the
playground.

"Wheeeeee!" said Natalie.
"This is wonderful! Can we go
right over the rooftops?"

"You bet!" said the monster.

They did twirlie-whirlies round
the chimney-pots.

"Now let's do swoopie-doopies," said the monster.

They swooped right down to the park.

The duck pond looked like a puddle from high in the sky, but when they got nearer and nearer . . .

. . . the ducks started to get bigger
and bigger.

"Quick! Fly up or they'll get
us!" said Natalie.

"Chicken," teased the monster.

"No – duck!" said Natalie.

They swooped up just in time,
leaving the ducks quacking
foolishly.

"I live near the park," said Natalie. "There's my house. Look, there's my mum and my little brothers!"

"Hey, do you want to see my mum and my little brothers?" said the monster.

"You bet!" said Natalie.
    "OK. Monster Planet, here we
come!"

Chapter Three

The flying saucer's wings grew immensely.

They flapped faster and faster and faster.

The flying saucer shot straight into the sky. It flew higher than the tallest buildings in the whole world . . .

. . . higher than the world itself,
away to a different planet
altogether.

Monster Planet.

"There it is!" shouted the
monster.

"It's little!" said Natalie.

"So are we," said the monster.

"I can see water," said Natalie.

"It's our seaside," said the monster.

"I can see lots of little monster people!" said Natalie.

They had wild hair and pointy teeth and sharp claws and long tails. But they didn't look fierce. They looked friendly.

"Shall we go for a sail?" said the monster.

"You bet!" said Natalie. "Hey, do you have dolphins?"

"Watch!" said the monster, and he whistled.

Six special monster dolphins leapt out of the water and whistled back.

The smiliest special monster dolphin gave Natalie a ride.

"That was wonderful," said
Natalie. "But I'm all wet now."

"We have special drying
dragons on the beach," said the
monster, parking the flying
saucer.

"Do you want the warm
dragon, the hot dragon, or the
special sauna dragon?" said the
monster.

"Just the warm one, please,"
said Natalie.

She was wonderfully warm in
seconds.

The monster had the special
sauna treatment and was so red-
hot he fried an egg on himself
and ate it!

"Do you want an egg too, Natalie?" said the monster.

"Maybe not an egg," said Natalie. "But I am starving."

"Do you want to go to McMonsters?" said the monster.

"You bet!" said Natalie.

Natalie ate a McMonster
burger. And another and another
and another.

Whenever she got thirsty she
went to the pretty pink fountain.
It was strawberry monster milk
shake!

"I think I'm full up now," said
Natalie.

"Let's go and look round the
shops," said the monster.

"I haven't got any money,"
said Natalie.

"No problem," said the
monster. "Monster money grows
on trees, look. Just help yourself!"

So Natalie and the monster picked a pocketful of monster money and went to the monster shopping centre.

There was a monster pet shop with monster dogs and monster cats and monster rabbits and monster hamsters and monster mice.

Natalie liked the monster birds best. She bought them all so she could let them out of their cages.

The monster birds flapped their wings and flew far away.

"Let's go in the sports shop," said the monster.

"Yes! I'll buy that football," said Natalie.

"Who do you support?" said the monster. "I like the Monster Marvels."

"Me too," said Natalie.

"Do you want to go to the match?" said the monster.

"You bet!" said Natalie.

The monster football stadium
was packed out.

Natalie and the monster got
specially shown to their seats.

"Up the Monster Marvels!"
yelled Natalie.

They all waved to her when
they ran onto the pitch.

"Come and kick off for us, Natalie," they shouted.

Natalie scored a stupendous goal.

"Hurray for Natalie!" shouted all the monsters, while she leapt in the air.

The monster took Natalie to meet his monster nan after the match.

Monster Nan made a great fuss of them both. She gave them hot chocolate to drink and cold chocolate ice-cream to eat — and lots and lots and lots of chocolate bars.

"Don't tell your mum or she'll fuss about your teeth," said Monster Nan.

"I want to see your mum and your little brothers," said Natalie.

"Right," said the monster. "Hop back on the flying saucer."

They flew over the monster's house.

"There they are! That's my monster mum. And my little monster brothers."

"My brothers are little monsters too!" said Natalie.

"Why aren't you at school, you bad little monster?" shouted his monster mum.

"Uh oh. School!" said the monster.

"Off you go!" said Monster Mum.

They flew to Monster School. The monster teacher had wild hair and pointy teeth and sharp claws and a long tail.

He looked very fierce.

He didn't look friendly.

"Where on earth have you been? And who is this strange girl?" said the monster teacher.

"She's my friend Natalie from another planet. We've whizzed back here from Earth," said the monster.

"You're telling stories again!" said the monster teacher. "You're in big trouble, little monster."

"Oh help!" said the monster. "Let's go, Natalie!"

They jumped back on the saucer.

"Planet Earth, ever so quickly, please!" said the monster.

The saucer flew down and down and down, all the way back to Earth . . .

. . . right above Natalie's school.

"I don't think I want to go
back," said Natalie. "I think I
might be in big trouble too. I'd
sooner stay with you and have
MONSTER FUN."

Chapter Four

"I don't want to say goodbye!" said Natalie.

"Don't worry. I'll come back," said the monster.

"Promise?" said Natalie.

"You bet!" said the monster.

Natalie got ready to jump off the saucer. Then she saw a HUGE monster.

"Aaaaah!" said Natalie.

"Miaow," said the huge monster.

"It's the school cat!" said Natalie. "But it's much bigger than me now."

"Shake my hand, silly," said the monster. "Then you'll grow big again."

Natalie clasped the monster's paw and immediately started growing again.

"Get off my saucer before I get squashed!" said the tiny monster.

Natalie jumped to the ground as she grew to her proper size.

She waved goodbye, stroked the cat, grabbed the dustpan and brush, and ran back to her classroom.

"Natalie!" shouted Mr Hunter. "Where on earth have you been?"

"I haven't been anywhere on Earth, Mr Hunter. Wait till I tell you," said Natalie.

She told everyone her story about Monster Planet. Everyone loved Natalie's story. Everyone but Mr Hunter.

"You're telling stories again, Natalie!"

Guess what. Natalie was in big trouble.

Natalie cheered up that afternoon. A special visitor came to the school. A story-teller.

She told the children stories about mice and clowns and princes and elephants and gingerbread men.

"And now I'll tell you my favourite story," said the story-teller. "It's all about monsters!"

"Once upon a time there was this very, very, very tiny monster with wild hair and pointy teeth and sharp claws and a long tail. This tiny monster had his very own flying saucer," said the story-teller.

"That's Natalie's story!" said all the children. "Natalie's told us that story already, Miss."

"Come out here, Natalie. So you like telling stories?" said the story-teller.

"You bet!" said Natalie.

"Maybe you'll be a story-teller like me when you grow up."

"Do you want to tell the Monster Story, Natalie?" said the story-teller.

"Well, it is my story," said Natalie.

"It's my story too," said a teeny tiny voice.

So they all told the Monster Story together.

THE END

Jacqueline Wilson is one of Britain's bestselling contemporary authors, with 30 million books sold in the UK. She has been honoured with many major prizes for her work, including the Guardian Children's Fiction Award and the Children's Book of the Year. She is the author most often borrowed from libraries over the last decade.

Jacqueline is a former Children's Laureate, a professor of children's literature and in 2008 she was appointed a Dame for services to children's literacy.

Nick Sharratt knew from an early age that he wanted to use his drawing skills as his career, so he went to Manchester Polytechnic to do an Art Foundation course. He followed this up with a BA (Hons) in Graphic Design at St Martin's School of Art in London from 1981 to 1984.

Since graduating, Nick has worked full-time as an illustrator for children's books, publishers and magazines. His brilliant illustrations have brought to life many books, most notably the titles by Jacqueline Wilson.

Nick also writes books as well as illustrating them.

SLEEPOVERS

Amy, Bella, Chloe, Daisy and Emily
are friends at school and have their
own Alphabet Club (just look at their
initials!). The girls love having
sleepover parties for their birthdays.

But Daisy is worried – soon it
will be her turn. What will her friends
say when they meet her very
special big sister?

LIZZIE ZIPMOUTH

Lizzie refuses to speak. She doesn't want to talk to her new stepbrothers, Rory and Jake, or her new stepdad, Sam, or even her mum. Nothing at all can make her change her mind.

But Lizzie's about to meet another member of her new family who is just as quiet as Lizzie – Great-Gran. And she is even more stubborn!

THE WORRY WEBSITE

Holly, Greg, Natasha and all the other children in Mr Speed's class have different things to worry about. So Mr Speed sets up the Worry Website on the classroom computer – anyone can type in their problem, and other people can type in their own advice.

At least, that's the plan! But, as they find out, sometimes the best advice comes from the most unexpected place . . .

GLUBBSLYME

When Rebecca wades into the witch's pond after an argument with her best friend Sarah, she makes a very unusual new friend – a huge, warty toad! And Glubbslyme is no ordinary toad. He's hundreds of years old, he can talk, and best of all, he can work magic.

Maybe, just maybe, he can help Rebecca and Sarah to be best friends again . . .

THE DINOSAUR'S PACKED LUNCH

Dinah feels sad. Her class has gone on
a school trip to see the dinosaurs at the
museum, and everyone else has a tasty
packed lunch – except Dinah. Until
a funny new friend decides to help . . .

Soon Dinah has a very special
packed lunch – but there is an even
bigger surprise in store!

COLOUR FIRST READER